Piglet Meets A Heffalump

One day, Christopher Robin said carelessly:
"I saw a Heffalump today, Piglet."
"I saw one once," said Piglet. "At least I think I did."

"So did I," said Pooh, wondering what a Heffalump was like.

Then they talked about something else, until it was time for Pooh and Piglet to go home.

As they came to the Six Pine Trees, Pooh said:
"Piglet, I have decided to catch a Heffalump."
Pooh waited for Piglet to say "How?" but Piglet
said nothing. The fact was Piglet was wishing
that *he* had thought of it first.

"I shall do it," said Pooh, "by means of a Trap.
It must be a Cunning Trap, so you will have
to help me, Piglet."
"How shall we do it?" said Piglet.
And they sat down to think it out.

Pooh's idea was that they should dig a Very Deep
Pit, and the Heffalump would come and fall in.
"Why would he fall in?" said Piglet.
Pooh said the Heffalump might be looking up at the
sky, wondering if it would rain, so he wouldn't see
the Very Deep Pit until he was half-way down it.

Pooh felt sure that a bear with a **Very Clever Brain** could catch a Heffalump if he knew the **right way.** "Suppose," he said to Piglet, "*you* wanted to catch *me*, **how** would you do it?"

"Well," said Piglet. "I should make a **Trap,** put a **Jar of Honey** in and you would **smell** it and go in after it, and –" "And I should **lick** round the edges first and then the middle and then –" said Pooh **excitedly.**

"Yes, well never mind about that," said Piglet.
"The first thing to think of is, What do
Heffalumps like? I should think haycorns,
shouldn't you?"

Pooh, who had gone into a happy dream, woke
with a start, and said Honey was a much more
trappy thing than Haycorns.
"All right, *I'll* dig the pit, while *you* go and get
the honey," said Piglet.
"Very well," said Pooh and he stumped off.

As soon as he got home, he took down a large jar
from the top shelf. It had HUNNY written on it.
He took a large lick. "Yes," he said, "it is. No
doubt about that!" and he gave a deep sigh.
Having made certain, he took the jar back to Piglet.

Piglet said, "Is that all you've got left?" and Pooh said, "Yes." Because it was. So Piglet put the jar at the bottom of the Pit and they went off home together. "Good night," said Piglet. "And we meet at six o'clock tomorrow morning and see how many Heffalumps we've got in our Trap."

Some hours later, Pooh woke up. He was hungry.
He went to the larder, stood on a chair and reached
to the top shelf and found – nothing.
"That's funny," he thought. "I know I had a jar of
honey there. Then he began murmuring a murmur
to himself:

It's very, very funny,
'cos I know I had some honey;
'cos it had a label on,
Saying HUNNY.

A goloptious full-up pot too,
And I don't know where it's got to,
No, I don't know where it's gone—
Well, it's funny.

Suddenly he remembered. He had put it into the Cunning Trap. He got back into bed but he couldn't sleep. He tried counting Heffalumps but every Heffalump was making straight for Pooh's honey, *and eating it all*. Pooh could bear it no longer. He jumped out of bed and ran to the Six Pine Trees.

In the half-light the Very Deep Pit seemed deeper. Pooh climbed in. "Bother!" said Pooh, as he got his nose inside the jar. "A Heffalump has been eating it!"

And then he thought a little and said, "Oh, no *I did*. I forgot." But there was a little left at the very bottom and he pushed his head right in, and began to lick . . .

By and by Piglet woke up. He didn't feel very
brave. What was a Heffalump like? Was it Fierce?
Wouldn't it be better to pretend he had a headache,
and couldn't go to the Six Pine Trees? But suppose
it was a very fine day, and there was no Heffalump
in the Trap, here he would be, simply wasting his
time for nothing. What should he do?

Then he had a Clever Idea. He would go now,
peep into the Trap and see if there was a Heffalump
there. If there was, he would go back to bed, and
if there wasn't, he wouldn't. So off he went.

As he got nearer he could hear it heffalumping about like anything.

"Oh, dear, oh, dear, oh, dear!" said Piglet to himself. He wanted to run away but felt he must just see what a Heffalump was like. So he crept to the side of the Trap and looked in . . .

And all the time Winnie-the-Pooh had been trying
to get the honey-jar off his head. He tried bumping
it against things and tried to climb out of the Trap,
but couldn't find his way. At last he lifted his head,
jar and all, and made a roaring noise of Sadness
and Despair . . . and it was at that moment that
Piglet looked down.

"Help, help!" cried Piglet. "Horrible Heffalump!" and he scampered off as hard as he could. He didn't stop crying and scampering until he got to Christopher Robin's house.

"Whatever's the matter?" said Christopher Robin.
"Heff," said Piglet, "a Heff – a Heff – a Heffalump."
"What did it look like?"
"It had the biggest head you ever saw. A huge big – I don't know – like an enormous nothing. Like a jar."
"Well," said Christopher Robin, "I shall go and look at it. Come on."

"I can hear it, can't you?" said Piglet anxiously,
as they got near.
"I can hear something," said Christopher Robin.
It was Pooh bumping his head against a tree-root.
"There!" said Piglet. And he held on tight to
Christopher Robin's hand.

Suddenly Christopher Robin began to laugh . . .
And while he was still laughing – Crash went the
Heffalump's head against the tree-root, Smash
went the jar, and out came Pooh's head again . . .

Then Piglet saw what a Foolish Piglet he had
been, and he was so ashamed that he ran straight
home and went to bed. Christopher Robin and Pooh
went home to breakfast together.

"Oh, Bear!" said Christopher Robin.
"How I do love you!"
"So do I," said Pooh.

THIS STORY TOOK PLACE